TiME ★ TWiSTERS

NEIL ARMSTRONG AND NAT LOVE SPACE COWBOYS

ALSO BY STEVE SHEINKIN

TIME★TWISTERS

NEIL ARMSTRONG AND NAT LOVE SPACE COWBOYS

STEVE SHEINKIN

ROARING BROOK PRESS

Text copyright © 2019 by Steve Sheinkin

Illustrations copyright © 2019 by Neil Swaab

Published by Roaring Brook Press

Roaring Brook Press is a division of Holtzbrinck Publishing Holdings Limited Partnership

175 Fifth Avenue, New York, NY 10010

mackids.com

Library of Congress Control Number: 2018936545

Hardcover ISBN: 978-1-250-14897-1

Paperback ISBN: 978-1-250-15258-9

Our books may be purchased in bulk for promotional, educational, or business use. Please contact your local bookseller or the Macmillan Corporate and Premium Sales Department at (800) 221-7945 ext. 5442 or by email at MacmillanSpecialMarkets@macmillan.com.

First edition, 2019

Book design by Neil Swaab

Printed in the United States of America by LSC Communications, Harrisonburg, Virginia

Hardcover: 10 9 8 7 6 5 4 3 2 1

Paperback: 10 9 8 7 6 5 4 3 2 1

*For anyone who had to read a
history textbook I worked on—this
book is my apology!*

CHAPTER ONE

One summer day a spaceship appeared in the sky above Texas.

A teenage cowboy named Nat Love gazed up at the craft. It looked like a giant metal spider, with smoke shooting from its feet. Love rubbed his eyes, *sure* he was dreaming.

The year was 1869. Just to be clear, there were no spaceships in 1869.

At least, there weren't supposed to be.

Nat Love looked up again. The flying spider was still up there, rocking and tilting as it swooped down toward the plains.

Nat was about to call out to the other cowboys, but saw there was no need. They were all staring up, pointing, mouths open in shock. Hundreds of startled longhorn cows started pawing the ground and sniffing loudly.

"Easy," Nat called to the cattle. "Easy there, girls. It's nothing but a . . . well . . ."

He had no idea what to tell them.

The spaceship landed in the grass, kicking up a huge cloud of dust. The terrified cows took off running in all directions.

Nat groaned. It would take half the day to round the herd up again.

But first things first. What was this thing that had just dropped out of the sky?

Nat and the other cowboys rode toward the ship. It was about twenty feet high, with four long legs, covered in shiny metal. On one side was an American flag. But with too many stars. The flag Nat was used to seeing had thirty-seven stars. This one had—he counted them up quickly—fifty.

A *CLANK* came from inside the spaceship. Then a loud *WHOOSH* of rushing air.

"Look out, boys!" Nat yelled as a hatch on the side of the ship swung open.

Someone—some kind of space alien, Nat figured—backed out of the hatch. It was wearing a puffy white suit and a huge helmet. It climbed slowly down a ladder attached to one of the ship's long legs. As the alien hopped from the bottom of the ladder to the grass, it said:

The alien stopped and looked around. Its face was covered by a gold-tinted visor, but Nat could tell it was surprised by what it was seeing. Cowboys on horses, that is, and grass to the horizon.

"Houston," it said. "We've got a problem."

"Looking for Houston, mister?" Nat Love said. "You're about three hundred miles off course."

The alien looked right at Nat. Nat saw his own reflection in the alien's visor.

Another alien popped its head out of the spaceship. It said, "I told you, you should have let me fly."

"I'm not sure that was the problem," the first alien said. It reached up and started to pull off its helmet.

The cowboys yanked their horses back.

But inside the alien's helmet was a pretty normal-looking human. Late thirties, blue eyes, brown hair.

"Sorry to drop in like this," the man said.

He pointed to the man coming down the ladder.

the second man said, hopping to the ground.

"We're American astronauts," Armstrong said.

That meant nothing to the cowboys.

"Astronauts, you know," Buzz said, pointing up. "We fly to space?"

The cowboys stared at the astronauts.

The astronauts stared at the endless plains of grass.

"Let me take a wild guess," Neil Armstrong said. "This is not the moon."

CHAPTER TWO

"**O**kay, guys!" Ms. Maybee sang out to her fourth-grade class. "Who thinks it sounds like fun to go to the moon?"

"I'd rather go to lunch," Doc said.

Most of the kids laughed. Even Ms. Maybee smiled a little.

"I hear you, Doc," she said, "but first we're going to do something even better. We're going to read about history!"

The kids didn't moan and groan, like they usually did when it was time to study history. Reading about space sounded pretty cool.

Also, some very strange things had been happening in history lately.

Ms. Maybee held up her copy of the history textbook. "Today we'll read about the first people to walk on the moon, American astronauts Neil Armstrong and Buzz Aldrin."

Kids opened their books.

Doc turned to his stepsister, Abby. They both looked worried.

"So yesterday we read about the liftoff," Ms. Maybee said. "Neil, Buzz, and Michael Collins climbed into *Apollo 11*, which sat on top of a rocket nearly four hundred feet tall. The rocket blasted off from Cape Canaveral, Florida, zooming the astronauts into space at over twenty thousand miles per hour. As each stage of the rocket burned up its fuel, it fell away, splashing into the ocean. And *Apollo 11* began its three-day journey to the moon."

LAUNCH ESCAPE ASSEMBLY

COMMAND MODULE

SERVICE MODULE

LUNAR MODULE

THIRD STAGE

SECOND STAGE

FIRST STAGE

ENGINES

But it wasn't aimed at the moon—can anyone guess why not?

"The moon's always moving," Maya said. "It's orbiting Earth."

"Right!" Ms. Maybee said. "So the engineers at NASA—that's the agency in charge of our space program—they had to figure out exactly where the moon *would* be in three days. They had to hit a moving target from two hundred forty thousand miles away. Incredible, right?"

"How'd the astronauts go to the bathroom?" Carter asked.

Ms. Maybee sighed. "Seriously?"

"No, it's just, there's no gravity in space," Carter said. "So how do you keep, um, you know, *stuff*, from floating around?"

"Okay, I see your point," Ms. Maybee said. "We'll come back to that. Let's get to the most famous moment of all—the moon landing. Abby, will you read for us please?"

Abby read aloud.

"On July 20, 1969, Neil Armstrong and Buzz Aldrin crawled into the lunar module, called the *Eagle*. Michael Collins stayed behind in the command module, the *Columbia*. The lunar module separated from *Columbia*. With Armstrong at the controls, *Eagle* fired its engines and flew toward the surface of the moon."

"This part gives me goose bumps every time," Ms. Maybee said.

Abby continued. "Moments later, an alarm rang. Warning lights flashed. The computers on *Eagle* were crashing! Armstrong did not panic. He had years of experience as a pilot and astronaut. He was confident he could still land the ship on the moon.

"But then, suddenly, the lunar module disappeared. Gone. Just like that. No Neil. No Buzz. No *Eagle*."

Abby stopped reading.

"That's definitely not how I remember the story," Ms. Maybee said. "Where'd they go? I mean—spoiler alert—Neil Armstrong and Buzz Aldrin *did* land on the moon."

She looked up from her book.

CHAPTER THREE

Doc and Abby looked at each other.

Doc's dad had married Abby's mom about three years before. Doc and Abby spent so much time together, each could usually tell what the other was thinking.

Which, in this case, was:

Here we go again.

Doc started flipping through his textbook. "I bet they're in here somewhere."

"In where?" asked Ms. Maybee.

Doc stopped at the chapter called "Life in the Changing West." He read a few lines to himself. "Yep," he said. "I was afraid of that."

Abby read the same page in her book. She groaned.

"Doc? Abby?" Ms. Maybee said. "Do you have something you'd like to share?"

"Remember how we read about cowboys?" Abby said. "How their job was to move herds of cows from Texas all the way north to the railroad lines, so they could be shipped to cities in the East?"

"I remember," Ms. Maybee said.

"And there was that guy Nat Love?" Doc said. "Just fifteen when he started as a cowboy?"

"What about him?" their teacher asked.

"Okay, listen to this," Abby said. She read aloud:

"For cowboys like Nat Love, life was hard,

and often dangerous. On the cattle trails, Love spent sixteen hours a day on his horse, for three or four months at a time. He had to watch for venomous snakes, sudden storms, and flooding rivers. The greatest fear was a stampede—where cattle run wildly, crushing everything, and everyone, in their path. One thing Love never expected to see, however, was a spaceship. Yet one day a ship *did* appear in the sky above Texas. It landed on the grass. Two men in puffy white suits climbed down and asked directions to the moon. Yes, life for cowboys was exciting indeed!"

Abby stopped there.

"What's going on?" Maya asked. "First Abraham Lincoln comes to our school and becomes a pro wrestler."

"That was weird," Carter said.

"Yeah," Maddie said. "And then Abigail Adams leaves the White House to be a pirate in the Caribbean."

"That was weird," Carter said.

"So what's going on?" Maya asked. "What's wrong with history?"

Everyone turned to look at Doc and Abby.

"The thing is, history is broken," Doc said. "All mixed up. We mixed it. Me and Abby. And Abraham Lincoln."

"Not on purpose," Abby added.

"Actually, it's the whole class's fault," Doc said. "We kept saying, 'History is boring!' Well, Lincoln heard that and got mad and decided not to be in history anymore."

"That's when he showed up here as a pro wrestler," Abby said. "We tried to help fix things. And we sort of helped. But sort of made things worse. Anyway, now everyone in history knows they can do whatever they want."

Ms. Maybee shook her head, still very confused. "But that doesn't explain why Neil Armstrong and Buzz Aldrin landed in Texas instead of on the moon in 1969."

"It really doesn't," Abby agreed.

"We can fix it," Doc said.

"Later," Abby said to Doc. "After school."

"No, *now*," Doc said. "Things are getting out of control. He'd want us to go now."

"Who?" Maya asked.

"Abe Lincoln!" said Doc, jumping out of his chair.

"Sit down, Doc," Ms. Maybee demanded. "And tell us what you're talking about."

"I'm sorry, Ms. Maybee," Doc said. "It can't wait!"

"Doc!" Ms. Maybee shouted. "Where do you think you're—"

WHOOSH!

But he was already out the door.

CHAPTER FOUR

Doc raced down the hall and sped through the library, knocking over a stack of biographies Ms. Ventura was trying to shelve.

"I'm glad you're excited to find a book, but you need to—"

Doc didn't wait to hear the rest of the sentence. He sprinted past Ms. Ventura and burst into the small storage room in the back of the library. The room had bookshelves, stacks of boxes, a table, and two chairs.

And a tall cardboard box with just a few history books at the bottom.

As Doc and Abby had discovered, the box was some sort of portal or time machine—it took them to times and places they'd read about in class. Doc had no idea how it worked, and no time to think about it. He leaped onto a chair, then onto the table, and then onto a tall stack of boxes. With a

YEE-HAW!

he soared across the room toward the cardboard box.

He hit the top feet first and fell into the box.

And tumbled to earth on the plains of Texas. In the summer of 1869.

He stood and looked around. It was pretty much what he'd expected—grass, cows, men on horses. And, a mile in the distance, a spaceship shaped like a giant spider.

They don't call it the "Wild West" for nothing.

MOOOOO???

Doc had expected that, too.

He walked toward the ship, wondering if now might be a good time to start making a plan.

———————•———————

Over at the lunar module, the cowboys' trail boss was glaring at Neil Armstrong and Buzz Aldrin, furious with them for scaring off his cattle.

The astronauts were still trying to figure out where they were. And *when.*

"What did you say the date was?" Armstrong asked.

"July 20," the trail boss grunted.

"That's right," Buzz said. "July 20 is right."

"In the year 1869," Nat Love added.

"Wait, did you say *eighteen*?" Armstrong asked.

"It should be *nineteen*," Buzz said. "*1969.*"

The boss's face turned even redder. "Look, ain't you fellers kinda old to be playin' dress-up?"

"You think we should just try taking off?" Neil asked Buzz.

"The sooner the better," Buzz said.

"You boys ain't goin' nowhere," the trail boss said.

"We're in kind of a hurry," Buzz said.

"The whole world's expecting us," Neil said. "On the moon, I mean."

"That's *yer* problem," the boss barked. "You go when I say you go, got it?"

"Roger," Buzz said.

"The name's *Burt*," snapped the boss, "not Roger."

"Roger," Buzz said.

"Means, 'got the message.'" Neil explained.

The boss threw up his hands. "Enough of yer nonsense!" Turning to the other cowboys, he hollered, "Boys! Bring over our meanest mustangs!"

Then he got right up in the astronauts' faces, growling,

We're gonna see what you two tenderfoots are made of.

CHAPTER FIVE

Doc peeked out from behind the cowboys' wagon.

He saw Neil and Buzz surrounded by cowboys. Two other cowboys were pulling a pair of horses toward the group. The horses were kicking and snorting, fighting every inch of the way.

NOT FROM AROUND HERE, PARTNER?

Startled, Doc turned toward the voice. It had come from behind him.

He looked up at a very tall cowboy. A cowboy whose clothes were a little too small

on him. A cowboy with a beard, but no
mustache.

Okay, he wasn't a cowboy. He was
Abraham Lincoln.

Oh, good.
It's you.

Lincoln smiled,
tipping his hat.

Howdy.

Doc pointed to the lunar module sitting in
the grass. "What's going on here?"

Lincoln's smile faded. "Doc, I wish I knew,"

he said. "These astronauts are serious about their missions. They wouldn't have come here on purpose. It's almost as if . . . as if someone else did it."

"Purposely mixed things up?"

"I don't even want to think about it," Abe said. "The important thing now is to get Neil and Buzz back in their ship and on their way. The whole world's going to be watching that moon landing. We need to make sure it actually happens."

"We'll think of something," Doc said. "Soon, I hope."

Neil Armstrong and Buzz Aldrin, in space suits, each sat atop a grunting, furious horse.

"Okay, boys!" the trail boss shouted. "Let 'er rip!"

The cowboys holding the horses let go— and the horses jumped and kicked, trying to toss the riders. They whipped their heads around, snapping their jaws at the astronauts.

Neil and Buzz flopped around like puppets—but hung on.

The horses gradually gave in. They stood, snorting air out of their nostrils. Neil and Buzz hopped off their horses and stood, panting and sweating, on wobbly legs.

"You boys'll do," the trail boss snarled. "Yer hired. We head out in five minutes!"

Nat Love rode up and held out his canteen. "You guys did great!"

"Thanks," Buzz said. He took a long drink of water. "That kind of reminded me of astronaut training."

Neil drank and nodded. "Remember the vomit comet?"

Buzz laughed. "*Do* I."

"Vomit comet?" Nat asked. "Name of a horse?"

"I *wish*," Buzz said. "No, it was part of our training. They'd stick us in this big plane."

"They don't have airplanes here," Neil pointed out.

"A flying machine," Buzz said, holding out

his arms. "With wings. It would climb high and then dive. Over and over. For two hours."

"Each loop produces twenty seconds of weightlessness, and you float in the plane," Neil said. "Supposed to prepare you for being in space."

"Mostly, it prepares you to barf," Buzz said.

"Sounds like my kind of ride," Nat said. "But when you say 'space' . . . you mean, up in the sky? To the stars?"

"Not that far," Neil said. "Just to the moon."

Nat whistled with wonder.

The moon! You boys flew to the moon?

"Almost," Neil said. "We were trying to land when we suddenly, um, showed up here."

Neil and Buzz looked over to the lunar module. It was tied tight to the trunk of a tree. A couple of cowboys sat on their horses nearby, keeping watch.

"How do we get back up there?" Buzz wondered.

Neil shook his head. "I thought we trained for everything."

"Me too," Buzz said. "Somehow, we never practiced landing in Texas in 1869."

CHAPTER SIX

That's when Abraham Lincoln and Doc walked up.

"Howdy, gents," Lincoln said to Neil and Buzz. "It's me, Abraham Lincoln."

"President during the Civil War," Doc said.

The astronauts looked at each other.

"No time to explain," Lincoln said. "But here's the plan. I distract the cowboys, you make a run for your ship. Got it?"

The astronauts were far too confused to speak.

The trail boss rode up, howling, "Let's move out! Don't have all day!"

Abe Lincoln stepped forward. "You the boss of this outfit?"

The boss glared down from his horse. "Who's askin'?"

"They call me Old Abe. This here's my partner, Doc."

Doc tipped his baseball cap.

"We're looking to hire on as hands," Lincoln said.

"That so?" the boss said. "You look like a couple of greenhorns to me."

"Sir, I've been riding horses all my life," Lincoln said.

Which was true.

"I once rode a pony at a birthday party," Doc said.

Which was also true.

Doc didn't mention that the pony was the size of a large dog. Or that his dad held his hand the whole time.

The boss looked Lincoln up and down. "You're too tall for a cowboy," he said. "A big man is hard on a horse."

"Try me," Lincoln said.

The boss grinned an evil grin.

HECTOR! BRING OVER BAD-EYE!

The other cowboys laughed and gathered around. The men who'd been guarding the ship rode over for a closer look.

Lincoln winked to Neil and Buzz. So far, so good.

———————•———————

"Careful, Abe," Abby whispered. "You too, Doc. Though, honestly, you don't seem to be helping much."

Abby knew they couldn't hear her. But it was like she was with them—everything they did showed up on the pages of her history book.

Hers and everyone else's.

"This is incredible!" Ms. Maybee said. "Are you guys reading this?"

The class leaned forward, listening to every word, as Ms. Maybee read aloud:

"It took three cowboys to hold Bad-Eye still while Abraham Lincoln mounted the horse. Lincoln's long legs dangled nearly to the ground. The moment the cowboys let go, Bad-Eye bucked wildly, kicking his hind legs high off the ground, sending Abe soaring."

Abby listened with her head in her hands.

"Cowboys hooted and laughed as our sixteenth president sailed across camp, crashing head first into the side of the chuck-wagon. Nat Love and the boy named Doc rushed over to help Lincoln. Meanwhile, Neil Armstrong and Buzz Aldrin made a run for their lunar module. Well, really more of a waddle; it was impossible to run in their bulky space suits. They had gone only a few steps when the trail boss rode up and blocked their path. Lincoln's plan had failed. Miserably. Not even close."

There was a moment of silence—then a burst of questions.

"Why is Lincoln pretending to be a cowboy?"

"Is that kid really Doc? *Our* Doc?"

"How'd he get in the book?"

"Can we read more history?"

"One at a time, guys," Ms. Maybee said.

Abby stood up.

"Ms. Maybee," she said. "I need to go. To the library."

"Sit down, Abby," the teacher said.

"But I'm worried about Doc. I really need to—"

SIT! Ms. Maybee shouted. She never shouted.

Abby sat.

"No one leaves this room," Ms. Maybee said.

Not until I figure out what's going on here.

CHAPTER SEVEN

SOMEONE HAD BETTER TELL ME WHAT'S GOING ON!

That was the president of the United States, Richard Nixon. He was not pleased.

It was July 20, 1969—the day Neil Armstrong and Buzz Aldrin were supposed to land on the moon. Nixon was pacing the Oval Office in the White House in Washington, DC. He was on the phone with NASA's Manned Spacecraft Center in Houston, Texas, where a team of engineers and scientists controlled every detail of the flight to the moon.

But at the moment, they were just as confused as everyone else.

"Mr. President," said Gene Kranz, the mission's flight director, "as near as we can tell, there was some kind of computer glitch. We're working to resolve it."

"I'm sure you are," said Nixon. "But where are Neil and Buzz? Where's the *Eagle*?"

"We're not certain, sir," Kranz said. "We're trying to reach them by radio."

"Shouldn't they have landed by now?" Nixon asked.

"Ideally, yes," Kranz said. "But those men know their stuff, sir. They'll find a way."

"I certainly hope so," Nixon said. "Meanwhile, a billion people are tuning in to watch me phone the American astronauts. I'm gonna look pretty foolish if I call the moon and no one answers."

"I understand, Mr. President."

"What am I supposed to do? Leave a message with a Martian?"

"That seems unlikely, sir."

"Just find the *Eagle*!" Nixon said. "Understood?"

———•———

The *Eagle* was actually pretty easy to find. If you happened to be on the plains of west Texas in the summer of 1869.

Doc sat on the grass, about a hundred yards from the craft. He kept hoping Abby would suddenly appear. Abe Lincoln was next to him, leaning against a wagon wheel, holding a wet rag to his tender forehead.

Before leaving to round up the cattle, the trail boss had ordered Doc and Lincoln to cook supper for everyone.

Lincoln pushed himself up and looked in the back of the chuck wagon. It was packed with wooden crates, clay jars, and iron pots and pans.

"I don't do much cooking," Lincoln said. "What do you know how to make?"

"Lots of things," Doc said.

"Good."

"Popcorn. Pizza. Hot dogs. Waffles."

"Sounds delicious," Lincoln said. "Those men'll be hungry when they get back."

Doc got up and looked in the wagon.

"Okay," he said. "Where's the microwave?"

CHAPTER EIGHT

Nat Love and Neil Armstrong rode side by side as the sun sank low in the west. Buzz Aldrin followed a few yards behind.

Neil and Buzz were wearing blue flight suits—they'd left their space suits in the lunar module. The cowboys had rounded up the herd and were on their way back to camp.

Wow, this horse is bumpy! And I thought **fighter jets** had turbulence!

"That was brutal," Neil said, wiping sweat from his brow.

Nat laughed. "Just another day on the trail."

Neil looked over at Nat. "Aren't you young for this kind of work?"

"I was born in Tennessee, into slavery," Nat said.

"That's amazing," Neil said.

"Wouldn't want any other job," Nat said. "Except maybe yours."

"Well, if you can handle it out here, you've got the right stuff to be an astronaut."

"Flying through space, walking on the moon," Nat said, smiling. "I'd like to try it. Anyone been to the moon before?"

"Nope," Neil said. "Buzz and I were supposed to be the first. We—the United States—we're in this race with Russia, a 'space race,' people call it."

"And I take it the US and Russia ain't friends?"

"No, we're not," Neil said. "But they're good. They put the first satellite into space. The first man. The first woman. Now we're racing to be first to the moon. With the whole world watching. Looks like we're going to lose this one, too."

"We won't," Nat said. "Not if I can help it."

47

Doc did not find the microwave.

Turns out, cowboys didn't have microwaves.

Lincoln got a campfire going, and Doc poured ingredients that seemed like they might possibly make corn bread into an iron skillet. He loaded another pan with bacon and set them both by the flames. Abe Lincoln was in charge of the coffee.

It was getting dark when the cowboys rode wearily back into camp.

The trail boss sniffed the air. "What in tarnation have you fellers been cookin'?"

"Corn bread and bacon," Doc said. "Isn't that the usual cowboy meal?"

"Suppose so," the boss grumbled. "But it sure don't smell right. All right, boys," he called to the crew, "let's get some grub!"

The men hopped off their horses and carried metal plates and cups over to the fire. Neil and Buzz were with the group.

Nat Love was not.

"No sudden moves, boys," the boss warned the astronauts. "I've got more work for you yet."

"That's fine," Neil said. "Boy, I sure am hungry."

"Same here," Buzz agreed. "It'll be nice to eat something that doesn't come out of a tube."

"Fresh corn bread coming up!" Doc said.

49

He wrapped a cloth around the handle of the skillet and pulled it from the fire. He stuck a fork into the bread—but couldn't pull it back out.

"A little help?" he said.

Lincoln yanked the fork. The whole wheel of bread came out of the pan, stuck to the top of the fork like the world's worst lollipop.

"Anyone care for a nibble?" Abe asked. "I can pass it around."

The trail boss leaned forward and tapped on the bread. It sounded like he was knocking on a wooden door.

"Come in!" Doc said.

No one laughed.

"Okay, well, ah . . . who wants some bacon?" Doc asked. "Hope you like it crispy!"

Doc set down the pan of bacon. Floating in grease were what appeared to be black twigs.

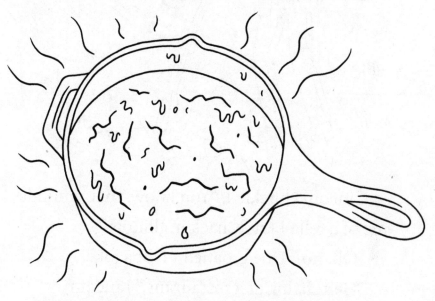

"Ain't there no coffee, at least?" groaned one of the men.

"There certainly is," Lincoln said. "Made it myself!"

He poured the cowboy a cup of coffee.

The cowboy sipped—and spat onto the grass.

Lincoln chuckled. "You know, that reminds me of a fella I knew back in Illinois."

"Oh, no," Doc groaned. "Not a joke."

"He's sitting at a restaurant," Lincoln began, "and the waitress brings him a drink. He sips it and makes a sour face. The waitress comes over. The man holds up the cup and says, 'Ma'am, if this is coffee, bring me tea. If it's tea, bring me coffee.'"

No laughs. Just crickets.

Actual crickets.

And then, suddenly—

KRRR-KRRR-BOOM!

The sound came from the direction of the lunar module.

Everyone looked over. The ropes that had tied *Eagle* to the tree lay in the grass, in pieces.

Puffs of smoke shot from the bottom of the craft, and one of its feet started lifting off the ground.

Inside the *Eagle*, Nat Love stood at the controls.

CHAPTER NINE

"**N**eil! Buzz!" Nat shouted. "Hurry! I got your ship!"

Neil and Buzz leaped up and ran toward their spacecraft.

"Get 'em, boys!" the trail boss screamed.

The cowboys chased the astronauts. Lincoln dove onto three of the men, knocking them to the ground, wrestling all three at once in a cloud of dust.

Abe Lincoln really loved wrestling.

The trail boss swung his rope above his head, aiming to lasso Neil Armstrong. Doc grabbed the corn bread lollipop and slammed it into the boss's boot.

"*Yowwww!*" the boss wailed, dropping his rope.

The lunar module was a foot off the ground, rocking and bucking. Nat held the controls, knees bent for balance, eyes wide, a massive grin on his face.

Neil lunged for the ladder, grabbed the bottom rung, and scrambled in through the hatch. One of the cowboys jumped on the ladder and started climbing.

"Great job, Nat!" Neil shouted.

"It's fun!" Nat cried. "What's this thing do?"

"No, wait!"

The craft lifted higher and spun wildly. The cowboy sailed off the ladder, bowling down a few of his pals. That left a clear path for Buzz. He reached for the ladder—but it was too high off the ground.

Neil took control of the lunar module. Nat leaned out the hatch, dropping one end of his rope.

"Buzz!" Nat shouted. "Grab hold!"

But just as Buzz got hold of the rope, the trail boss charged up.

"Behind you!" Doc warned.

The boss slammed into Buzz, wrapping his arms around the astronaut. Buzz held tight to the rope.

"Here I come!" yelled Doc.

He grabbed the wheel of corn bread, tucked it under his arm, and ran.

The *Eagle* was still swaying, smoking, and sparking from its spider feet. Neil stood at the controls, flipping switches, watching the spinning dials.

"Can't hold it like this," he said. "We gotta go, Buzz! Gotta go!"

Buzz clung to the rope. The trail boss clung to Buzz. They were both off the ground, swinging on the end of the rope.

"Too much weight!" Neil called. "I can't lift it!"

"Quick!" Nat shouted, reaching his hand out to Buzz. "Get in, and I'll jump out!"

But Buzz couldn't shake free of the trail boss.

"Here I come!" yelled Doc.

He stopped, wound up, and threw the corn bread. It sailed toward the trail boss. But then the boss and Buzz spun around on the rope, and the bread was headed for Buzz.

"Look out!" Doc screamed.

Too late. Buzz never saw the corn bread coming.

The loaf smacked his back. He and the trail boss tumbled from the rope, landing hard in a muddy ditch.

Without the extra weight, the *Eagle* shot straight up—and disappeared.

Doc, Abraham Lincoln, Buzz Aldrin, and a bunch of very angry cowboys looked up into the night. All they could see was the starry black sky.

And the moon.

CHAPTER TEN

Doc and Abe Lincoln brushed dirt off their clothes.

Doc said, "You think maybe we should stop trying to fix history?"

"Too late now," Lincoln said. "Let's at least get Buzz out of that ditch."

They helped Buzz climb out of the mud.

Buzz looked up at the sky, shaking his head. "I wanted to be the first one on the moon," he mumbled. "Now I don't even get to be second."

Doc clapped Buzz on the back. "Look on the bright side."

"And what's that?" Buzz snapped.

"Give me a second," Doc said.

The cowboys surrounded Doc, Buzz, and Lincoln.

"I don't care where you fellers came from," the trail boss growled. "You work for *me* now."

"For how long?" Doc asked. "Because I have soccer later."

"For as long as I say, got it?" roared the boss. "Now pony up, all three of you. Yer on the night watch."

———————

It was lunchtime at Division Street Elementary, and Abby sat at a table in the cafeteria, hunched over her history textbook. She hadn't even touched her sandwich.

Must find a solution . . .

"Doc, Buzz Aldrin, and Abraham Lincoln sat on horses, watching the herd," Abby read in her book. "This was an easy enough job, most nights. But now a storm was rolling in from the north. Lightning flashed in the sky. The cattle—nervous animals by nature— were on their feet, grunting and bellowing. This was a dangerous moment. If even one cow began to run, the whole herd could stampede. The cowboys would be flattened like pancakes."

"Sing," Abby muttered to herself.

Sing!

"Who, me?" the kid next to Abby asked.

"No, them!" Abby shouted, slapping the page of her book.

It's how cowboys used to keep cattle calm at night. They'd sing to them!

She jumped up.

One of the lunch monitors strode over. "Where do you think *you're* going?"

"I'm done with lunch," Abby said. "Is it okay if I . . ." She wasn't sure what to say. She knew the question, "Is it okay if I go into history to save my brother, Buzz Aldrin, and Abraham Lincoln?" would sound kind of weird.

The lunch monitor stood with her arms crossed. "Take your seat."

"Look!" Abby shouted, pointing across the room. "Someone's eating his ice cream before his vegetables!"

The monitor spun around, furious. "Where? Put that down!" She stalked between tables, looking for the dessert eater.

Abby ran out of the cafeteria.

She darted down the hall, hurdled a kindergartner, and dashed by the front desk of the library.

"Did your brother find the book he was looking for?" Ms. Ventura asked.

"I'll ask!" Abby said as she flew past.

She stumbled into the storage room, climbed onto a pile of boxes, jumped into the tall cardboard box—

And came down on the plains of Texas in 1869. Surrounded by nervous longhorn cattle. They really did have very long horns. Pointy, too.

"Doc!" Abby shouted. She couldn't see far in the dark. "Doc!"

"Abby!" Doc called back. "Is that you?"

"Over here!" Abby answered.

Doc found Abby and helped her up.

"I'm here to help," Abby said.

"Me too," said Doc. "So far it's not working out."

Lincoln and Buzz ran over.

A flash of lightning lit the plains for an instant—all around, cows were starting to move as a group.

"What do we do?" Buzz asked.

"Sing," Abby said.

"Sing?" asked Lincoln.

"Sing!" Abby said again. "Cowboys sang to their herds at night."

BOOM!

"Right!" Doc said. "We learned that in music. What was that song?"

"The dogies!" Abby said.

Doc started:

AS I was a-walking one morning for pleasure, I spied a young cowpuncher a-riding alone.

Abby joined in:

His hat was throwed back and his spurs was a-jingling, As he approached me a-singing this song . . .

Doc and Abby had many talents. Singing wasn't one of them.

Buzz and Lincoln joined in. They were just as bad. Maybe even worse.

And at that exact moment, they disappeared. They didn't even get to finish the chorus.

CHAPTER ELEVEN

Buzz Aldrin, Doc, and Abby plopped down on a field of grass. No sign of Abe Lincoln. The air was wet and warm. Thunder rumbled in the distance.

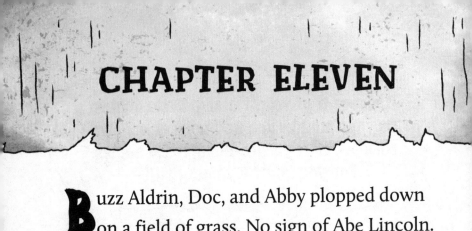

Now where are we?

I guess they kicked us out of history.

"Was our singing that bad?" Doc asked.

They stood and looked around. There were office buildings, with lights on in many of the windows. And parking lots full of cars. Cars from the 1960s.

"Looks like we're still in history," Abby said.

"Not *me*," said Buzz Aldrin. "This is Houston, the Manned Spacecraft Center." He laughed. "Funny thing is, this land used to be a cattle ranch."

"Busy night," Doc said. "Going by the full parking lots."

"The night of the moon landing?" Abby said.

"Must be," Buzz said.

"Sorry," Doc said. "I guess that's a sore subject."

"Forget it, kid," Buzz said. "Nothing matters now but the mission. The whole world is watching. The mission *must* succeed."

"We're here to help," Abby said.

"Even if it's hard to tell," Doc said.

"Mission Control's in there," Buzz said, pointing to a nearby building. "We need to find out what's going on. Follow me!"

Neil Armstrong gripped the controls of the lunar module. Nat Love stood beside him in the tiny craft.

Alarms rang and yellow warning lights flashed. The craft's computers were overloaded and useless. Neil looked out the window to his left. The good news—that was the moon down there. Not Texas. They were about ten thousand feet above the surface and dropping fast.

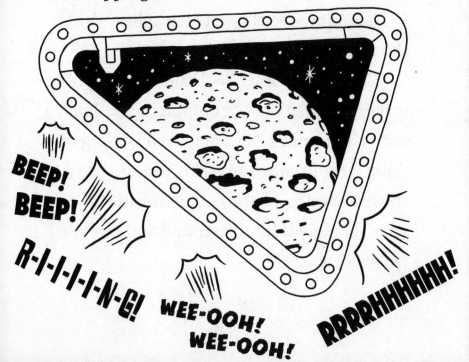

BEEP!
BEEP!

R-I-I-I-I-N-G!

WEE-OOH!
WEE-OOH!

RRRRHHHHHH!

A scratchy voice came over the radio: "*Eagle*, this is Houston. Do you read? Over."

There was a pause, and then the voice repeated: "*Eagle*, Houston. Do you—"

Neil flicked a switch, shutting off the radio.

"We'll talk to Houston in a minute," he said.

"Might be tough to explain what I'm doing here," Nat said.

Neil nodded. "That's what I'm thinking. But look, I came here to land on the moon. You up for it?"

Nat pointed to the warning lights. "What about these?"

"Computer crash," Neil said. "It's okay. A real pilot doesn't need computers." He looked at Nat and smiled. "I've practiced landing this thing lots of times. On Earth, I mean. Only crashed it once. I bailed out two-fifths of a second before it hit the ground and exploded. No big deal."

Nat's heart was pounding. He'd left home seeking adventure. Here it was.

"Let's land," he said. "How can I help?"

"See that gauge there?" Neil said, pointing to the panel of instruments. "That's our altitude. That one's the fuel. When I ask, you read them out, okay?"

"Got it."

"Hang on," Neil said.

IT'S GONNA GET BUMPY.

CHAPTER TWELVE

Buzz, Doc, and Abby hurried through the halls of the Mission Control center. People were rushing around, too busy to notice Buzz or the kids. Which was lucky, since the kids had no business being there.

And Buzz was supposed to be on the moon.

Buzz led them to a wall of windows. On the other side of the glass was the huge Mission Control room.

"They lock the doors during missions," Buzz whispered. "So no one distracts the guys inside. But family members, off-duty astronauts, VIPs—they can watch from here."

Buzz pointed. About twenty men and women were watching through the glass.

Inside Mission Control, a huge team of

specialists sat at long tables, talking into headsets, flipping through binders, pushing buttons, watching data flash across their screens.

"What are they all doing?" Doc asked.

"All different jobs," Buzz said. "Rocket scientists, computer techs, engineers, even doctors monitoring the astronauts' heart rates. See the guy with the vest? That's Charles Duke. He's the 'CapCom'—the capsule communicator. Only *he* talks directly to the astronauts."

Charles Duke spoke into the microphone on his headset. His voice was broadcast through speakers on the wall.

"*Eagle*, this is Houston," Duke said. "Do you read? Over."

There was no answer.

"*Eagle*, this is Houston," Duke said. "Do you read? Over."

Duke sounded calm—but his face was tight, worried.

Flight director Gene Kranz banged his desk. "Where *are* these guys?"

"*Eagle*, Houston," Duke said. "Do you read? Over."

No answer.

"Come on, people!" Kranz called out. "The president wants answers! I've got newspapers and TV stations demanding updates! Janet Armstrong and Joan Aldrin want to know where their husbands are! Anyone have anything? *Anything?*"

No one did.

"*Eagle*, Houston," Duke said. "Do you read? Over."

Doc and Abby looked at each other.

"Come on, Neil," Buzz urged, clenching his fists. "Come on . . ."

"Altitude?" Neil called.

"Two thousand feet," Nat said. "Falling fifty feet per second."

Neil checked the view from his window—and didn't like it. The plan had been to land on a section of the moon called the Sea of Tranquility. It looked nice and flat in photos. Now, up close, Neil saw that the planned course was taking them into a crater the size of a football stadium.

DESTINATION

UH-OH!

"One thousand feet," Nat said.

"Fuel?"

"Sixty seconds of fuel," Nat said.

They zipped past the crater, skimming over car-size boulders, looking for a place to land.

"Forty seconds of fuel," Nat said.

"Look," Neil said. "That's our spot."

"Thirty seconds."

"Roger."

"Forty feet," Nat said. "Thirty feet. Twenty."

Its thrusters kicking up gray dust, *Eagle*'s long spider-like legs set down on the surface of the moon. The dust settled quickly.

Suddenly, it was dead quiet in the *Eagle*. No engine noise. No radio. No weather. No wind.

Neil Armstrong reached out his hand to Nat Love. "Welcome to the moon," he said as they shook.

"That was some ride," Nat said. "You'd make a good cowboy."

"Thanks, Nat. You'd make a good astronaut," Neil said. "In fact, you *are* one now. The world's going to be watching us, and they don't need to know that anything's gone wrong. Agreed?"

Nat smiled. "Just call me Buzz."

"Roger," Neil said.

And he flicked the radio back on.

CHAPTER THIRTEEN

Mission Control was tense and silent.

"*Eagle*, this is Houston," Charles Duke said into his headset. "Do you read? Over."

Still no answer.

Duke leaned forward. "*Eagle*, Houston. Do you read? Over."

A faint electric crackle broke the silence. Then came the voice of Neil Armstrong:

"Houston, Tranquility Base here. The *Eagle* has landed."

The entire room erupted in cheers.

WOO-HOO! YES! ALRIGHT!

"Yes!" Buzz roared.

Doc and Abby high-fived and did a dance.

All the other visitors looked over. They were happy, too. But not dancing.

Abby smiled at them. "That's my, um . . . uncle up there."

"Good old Uncle Buzz!" Doc said.

"Yeah, he's great," Buzz said, hiding his face behind his hand.

"Roger, Tranquility," Duke said. "You've

got a bunch of guys about to turn blue. We're breathing again."

"A little computer trouble during descent," Armstrong said.

"We noticed," Duke said. "How's Buzz?"

"Oh, ah . . ." Armstrong said. "He's good. Real good."

"Buzz?" Duke said. "You copy, Buzz?"

"Howdy, fellas!" said Nat Love.

The real Buzz Aldrin moaned. "Since when do I say howdy? I'm from New Jersey."

But it's hard to tell one voice from another from 240,000 miles away. No one in Mission Control suspected they were speaking to a teenage cowboy.

———————•———————

In the lunar module, Neil and Nat spent the next hour getting into space suits.

Buzz's suit fit Nat pretty well. Astronauts—like cowboys—were not big guys. In the 1960s, the average astronaut was five-foot-ten, 160 pounds. Any bigger, and they wouldn't have fit in the tight spaces inside early spacecraft.

"Do we really need all this stuff?" Nat asked.

"Wouldn't last long without it," Neil said. "There's no oxygen to breathe out there. It's over two hundred degrees in the sun and two hundred below zero in shadow. There are dust particles speeding through space faster than bullets. There's deadly radiation. And of course, no air pressure."

"Air pressure?" Nat asked.

"The weight of the air, basically," Neil explained. "You don't feel it on Earth, but it's there, pushing down on you. Out here there's no air, no weight. Without the pressure suits, the gas in our blood vessels would expand, and we'd puff up like balloons, and, well—it'd get pretty unpleasant."

"I'll wear the suit," Nat said.

"Good idea."

"What's this thing for?" Nat asked, pointing to a tube that fit around his waist.

"Collects your urine," Neil said.

"Boy, they think of everything."

"They sure do."

The men pulled on boots, gloves, and helmets. The gold-tinted visor would protect their eyes from the sun's bright rays—and make it impossible to see who was inside.

Which was lucky, given the circumstances. Neil asked,

"You should go first," Nat said.

"Don't mind if I do."

Neil Armstrong opened *Eagle*'s hatch and backed out. He put a boot on the ladder and began climbing down to the surface of the moon.

A camera attached to the outside of *Eagle* was rolling, sending grainy black-and-white images back to Earth. A billion people crowded around TV screens, watching Neil Armstrong back down the ladder. In all human history, no one had ever seen anything like this.

How amazing!

In Houston, the Mission Control team stared up at a huge screen on the wall.

Abby and Doc watched, open-mouthed with awe, through the glass.

This is so cool.

"This is it," Buzz whispered. "Careful . . ."

Neil's voice, distant and scratchy, came through the speakers on the wall. "I'm at the foot of the ladder."

"Roger," Charles Duke answered. "We copy."

"I'm going to step off now," Neil said.

And with a stiff-legged hop, Neil
Armstrong jumped down to the surface of the
moon.

"That's one small step for man, one giant
leap for

CHAPTER FOURTEEN

The team in Mission Control roared with joy. Men slapped each other on the back and waved American flags.

Buzz Aldrin whispered,

"What?" Abby asked.

"The *a*," Buzz said. "He practiced it a hundred times. It was supposed to be 'That's one small step for *a* man, one giant leap for mankind.'"

"It makes more sense with the *a*," Abby said.

"It does," Buzz said. "Neil's a pilot, not a public speaker."

"It's still a great line," Doc said.

"It's a classic," Buzz agreed. He smiled and clapped loudly. "We did it. We got to the moon!"

"We did!" Doc agreed. "Once again, we fixed history!"

"You think so?" Abby asked.

"Sort of," Doc said. "I mean, as far as anyone knows."

"I guess," Abby said.

Then she noticed two men in uniforms walking toward them. She nudged Doc, who nudged Buzz.

Buzz turned and ran down the hall.

The guards walked up to Doc and Abby.

What are you kids doing in here?

one of them demanded.

"We, uh . . ." Abby began. "Our uncle is, um . . ."

She looked down the hall in the direction Buzz had run. He'd ducked into an office and was safely out of sight.

The guard stuck out his open hand. "Let's see your visitor passes."

"I dropped mine," Doc said. "Can I have a new one?"

"Me too," Abby said.

"Come with us," the man ordered.

NOW.

In the lunar module, Nat Love coiled up his rope and tossed it over his shoulder. It was bad enough for a cowboy to be without his horse. He couldn't stand to be without the rope, too.

Then he backed down the ladder.

"Whoops!" he said. "I just locked us out."

"Please repeat, Buzz," Charles Duke said from Houston. "Locked out of what?"

"The door to the lunar thing," Nat said. "Who's got the key?"

Neil Armstrong spun around. The *Eagle*'s hatch was open. There was no lock on the outside, anyway.

"Very funny, Buzz," Neil said.

"Hilarious," said Duke. "Let's get to work, fellas."

Nat jumped to the ground and gaped at the lunar landscape. The dusty gray surface was dotted with rocks and craters, and it stretched to the horizon under an ink-black sky. It was beautiful, in a way. Kind of like a desert drained of color.

And it was easy to move around. The moon has just one-sixth the gravity of Earth—so everything weighs one-sixth as much. On Earth, the astronauts, with their heavy suits and packs, would have weighed 360 pounds. On the moon, they weighed just sixty. Neil and Nat quickly realized they could hop around like kangaroos.

They set up a TV camera, pointing it toward *Eagle*. This gave viewers on Earth a much clearer picture of the moon. In front of the camera, Neil and Nat planted the American flag. Or, they tried to. The flagpole wouldn't stand up in the shallow, dusty soil. They got on their knees and tried patting dirt around the base of the pole. It kept tilting over.

Come on, flag, straighten up or ship out.

"Tranquility Base, this is Houston," Duke said. "The president of the United States would like to say a few words to you. Over."

"Roger," Neil said. "Just let us get this flag set up."

He spotted a few small rocks at the edge of a nearby crater—just the thing to prop up the pole. He hopped to the crater, but got going too fast, and when he planted his boots to stop, he slid like a skier down the crater's steep, sandy slope.

Shouting

the whole way down.

"This is Houston. Say again, Neil."

"It's just I, um . . ." Neil began. "I saw a very exciting rock specimen."

"That's great, Neil," Duke said. "Could we get you and Buzz on camera, please?"

"Just a sec," Neil said.

He was standing in a crater the size of a swimming pool. The walls were six feet high.

"Buzz," he said,

Could you help me with this, um, rock?

Nat could see the footprints leading to the crater. "Coming, partner!"

He hopped over. Too fast.

"Be careful!" Neil called. "The edge is a bit slipper—"

Too late. Nat sand-skied into the crater.

"Hello, Neil and Buzz!" said President Richard Nixon. "Hello? Neil and Buzz?"

CHAPTER FIFTEEN

"**N**ow I can't see the astronauts," President Nixon groaned. "Where are they? You told me they were ready."

"They were, Mr. President," said Flight Director Kranz.

"This is Houston," Duke said. "Still with us, boys? We can't see you."

"We're here," Neil said.

"The president is waiting, Neil," Duke said.

"We copy," said Neil. "Stand by."

Nat took the rope off his shoulder—he *knew* it would come in handy. He tied a loop in one end and looked up for something to lasso. If he could get one end of the rope around something outside the crater, they could pull themselves out.

There was nothing. Just the sandy slopes

of the crater and the black sky.

Neil bent down and signaled for Nat to
climb on his shoulders. Nat lifted a leg over
Neil's back. Neil stood, wobbled, but didn't
fall. From this height, Nat could see a boulder
far in the distance. Too far to lasso. On Earth,
anyway. Here, in the moon's low gravity, it
might work.

Nat swung the rope around and around over his head and let it fly. It sailed and sailed and came down around the boulder.

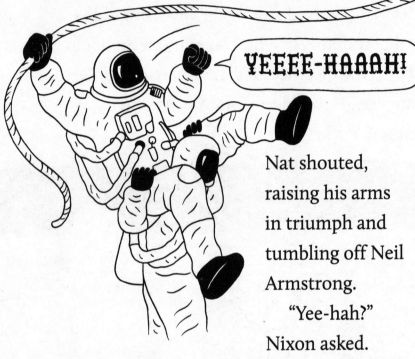

YEEEE-HAAAH!

Nat shouted, raising his arms in triumph and tumbling off Neil Armstrong.

"Yee-hah?" Nixon asked. "Does that mean they got the rock specimen?"

"Sounds like it, Mr. President," said Kranz.

Nat yanked the rope tight. He and Neil scrambled out of the crater.

They hopped to the TV camera and stood in front of *Eagle* and the American flag.

"Here they are," Duke said. "Go ahead, Mr. President."

"Hello, Neil and Buzz!" Nixon almost sang. "I am talking to you by telephone from the Oval Room at the White House, and this certainly has to be the most historical telephone call ever made!"

———•———

Abby and Doc watched it all on TV.

The guards had taken them to a small room. He told them to sit and wait. He locked them in. But at least there was a television.

They listened to Nixon's speech about how proud everyone was of the astronauts. Neil Armstrong thanked the president and said it was an honor to represent the United States and people of peace from all nations.

Then Nixon said something that Abby and Doc didn't quite understand: "I look forward to seeing you on the *Hornet* on Thursday."

The two astronauts looked at each other.

"We, uh, we look forward to that very much, sir," Neil said.

That was the end of the phone call.

"What does that mean?" Doc asked. "The *Hornet*? Thursday?"

"I don't know," Abby said. "But didn't Neil seem sort of worried when Nixon said it?"

"Hard to tell," Doc said. "We better find Buzz and—"

The door opened. A man with an official-looking badge clipped to his suit walked in and sat down.

"What did President Nixon mean?" Doc asked the man. "What's the *Hornet*?"

The man smiled coldly.

I'll ask the questions here.

CHAPTER SIXTEEN

The man opened a notebook and picked up a pen. "Has anyone called your parents?"

"That could be tough," Abby said.

"They don't have a phone?"

"No, they do," Abby said. "It's just . . . I'm not sure if they've been born yet."

The man looked up from his writing.

Abby and Doc sat there, with no idea what to say.

"How'd you get in here?"

"We know Buzz," Doc said.

"Aldrin?"

Doc nodded.

"Fine, but he couldn't have let you in." The man pointed to the TV. "In case you haven't noticed, he's on the moon."

"Obviously," Abby said.

"You kids are in serious trouble," the man said. He picked up a telephone and dialed. "It's me, sir," he said into the phone. "Yes, I'm with them now."

Abby leaned to Doc, whispering, "You thinking what I'm thinking?"

"If it's about getting out of here, yeah," Doc whispered. "Think it'll work again?"

"Worth a shot."

And they started to sing.

"That's them, sir," the man said into the phone. "Some sort of horrible cowboy song. Yes, sir, I'll ask them to stop."

But Abby and Doc kept singing.

Whoopee ti yi yo, git along, little dogies,
For you know Wyoming will be your—

And they disappeared.

"Okay, sir, they stopped," the man said. "But . . . well, this is going to sound a bit strange."

Neil Armstrong and Nat Love were back in the *Eagle*, ready to head home.

Neil fired *Eagle*'s ascent rockets—knocking over the flag he and Nat had gone to so much trouble to set up. The craft lifted off and docked with the command module, the *Columbia*. Michael Collins opened a hatch in *Columbia*, and Neil Armstrong crawled in. Followed by Nat Love.

"We'll explain later," Neil said when he saw the shocked look on Collins's face.

They released *Eagle*, which orbited the moon, then crashed to the surface. Collins fired the ship's rocket and they were on their way back to Earth.

The astronauts strapped into their seats to keep from floating in the zero gravity of space. They ate freeze-dried bacon and peaches and drank fruit punch from pouches. Neil and Mike showed Nat how to use the "bathroom." Peeing was easy—you held a tube that sucked the liquid into a bag. Pooping was much harder. You had to tape a bag to your rear end, and then, when you were done, remove it very carefully to keep anything from floating around the cabin.

Nat decided he could wait.

Neil and Nat told Mike their story, and they talked over what would happen when they got back to Earth. The plan was for the capsule to splash down in the Pacific Ocean. It would be picked up by an aircraft carrier, the *Hornet*.

"And the president will be there to greet us," Mike said.

"That's a problem," Nat noted. "I don't look much like Buzz."

They thought for a while.

"Well, not much we can do from here," Neil said. "Buzz and those kids—I'm sure they'll think of something."

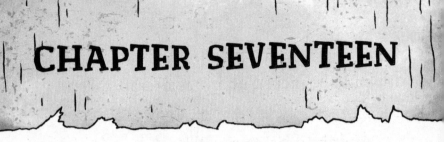

CHAPTER SEVENTEEN

Doc and Abby crashed down on a paved surface. A runway. A runway on the deck of a massive ship.

"I was sort of hoping that would get us home," Doc said.

"Guess we're not done yet," Abby said.

Planes and helicopters were parked at one end of the deck. The sun was rising, and there was ocean all around.

"We're on an aircraft carrier," Doc said.

"It's cool," Abby agreed, "but—"

That was the sound of someone else landing a few feet away.

It was Buzz Aldrin.

"It worked!" Buzz said. "Come on, let's get out of view."

They darted behind a plane.

"How'd you get here?" Doc asked.

"Same as you," Buzz said. "I was hiding in the hall, no idea what to do, when I heard this awful racket. It was you two singing!"

"Gee, thanks," Abby said.

"I tried it," said Buzz. "And *BAM!* Here I am, on the good old USS *Hornet*."

"*Hornet!*" Doc said. "Nixon said something about the *Hornet* and Thursday."

"Right," Buzz said. "The *Columbia* will splash down here Thursday morning."

"And President Nixon will be here to greet them," Abby said.

"Yep," Buzz said. "With TV cameras rolling, bands playing, the whole thing."

"We have to get Nat out of there!" Doc said.

"And you in," said Abby.

"We'll be fine," Buzz said. "The moon landing was Sunday night, Houston time. So we have plenty of time to—"

Buzz was interrupted by the *WHUMP-WHUMP-WHUMP* of a helicopter in the air above the aircraft carrier. Sailors ran to greet the chopper as it set down on the flight deck. Four men in dark suits jumped out.

"Secret Service," Buzz said.

The sailors stood at attention and saluted.

President Richard Nixon stepped out of the helicopter.

"Wasn't he just in the White House?" Abby asked.

"Could it be Thursday already?" Doc wondered.

"Must be," Buzz said, shaking his head.

"Man, I really don't understand this whole time-travel thing."

———————•———————

But Buzz was right—it was Thursday.

After a smooth flight back from the moon, the command module *Columbia* was about to re-enter Earth's atmosphere.

"Have a good trip," CapCom Charles Duke told the *Columbia* crew. "And remember to come in BEF."

"Roger that," Mike Collins said. "See you soon."

The astronauts strapped themselves tight into their seats.

"BEF?" Nat asked.

"Butt End Forward," Neil explained. "Ever fire a rifle?"

"Sure."

"A rifle bullet travels two thousand miles per hour," Neil said. "We're about to hit the atmosphere—the blanket of gases surrounding the planet—at twenty-six thousand miles per hour."

"That's why we fly BEF," Mike added. "If I can keep *Columbia*'s flat end in front, it should slow us down enough to keep from burning up. Hold on, here we go!"

The astronauts rattled and rocked, and flames shot from the back of *Columbia* as the outside of the craft reached five thousand degrees Fahrenheit. But the heat shields did their job.

Inside, it was a comfortable eighty degrees.

CHAPTER EIGHT

On the flight deck of the *Hornet*, sailors pointed at the sky and shouted.

"Look! They made it!"

"There they are, Mr. President!"

President Nixon looked up, smiling with amazement.

High above the ocean, three red-and-white parachutes drifted slowly down. Dangling below the chutes was the *Columbia* capsule.

Buzz, Doc, and Abby watched from their hiding place behind a plane.

"We just ran out of time," Abby said.

"Not yet," Buzz said. "We've got one last chance."

"What's that?" Doc asked.

"Moon germs," Buzz said.

"Huh?"

"Moon germs," Buzz repeated. "Doctors are worried the astronauts might bring home deadly germs from the moon. Possibly destroy all life on Earth."

"That would be bad," Abby said.

"Sure," said Buzz, "but it's our chance. The plan is to keep the men isolated until they can be tested. Hurry! Follow me!"

He sprinted across the flight deck, ducked through a doorway, and clattered down a metal flight of steps.

———————•———————

The *Columbia* splashed down, and flotation bags inflated on the outside of the craft. The capsule bobbed in the choppy sea.

Everyone on the *Hornet*—except Abby,

Doc, and Buzz Aldrin—watched from the edge of the deck.

A Navy diver paddled a raft to the capsule. With him in the raft were four BIGs— Biological Isolation Garments. The diver put on one of the gray full-body suits and the helmet and gas mask that went with it. Buzz was right—NASA was seriously worried about moon germs.

Columbia's hatch opened.

The diver lifted his mask from his mouth to say, "Welcome home, guys. It's a real honor to—*WHOA!*"

He was nearly knocked into the ocean by the smell wafting from the capsule.

"Hey, you try not washing for a week," Neil said.

"Yeah," Mike added. "And something about the freeze-dried food made us a little gassy."

The diver tossed in three BIGs and quickly shut the hatch—to keep in any moon germs.

And the stench. A few minutes later, the hatch opened again. Neil, Nat, and Mike climbed out, wearing the BIGs.

The helmets and gas masks completely covered their faces.

A helicopter hovered overhead. The crew

lowered a basket to carry the astronauts to the *Hornet*.

Aboard the ship, Abby and Doc raced after Buzz. He led the way to a large, open space below the flight deck. Rows of chairs were set up, and TV cameras sat on tripods. There were music stands and band instruments sitting on some of the empty chairs.

In front of the chairs was a trailer. A silver Airstream trailer, like you'd see being towed by a car on the highway. But without wheels.

"This is the Mobile Quarantine Facility,"

Buzz said. "The crew will be taken straight here, before anyone gets a good look at them."

"So we just need to hide you in there," Abby said.

"And get Nat out later," Doc said. "Easy."

Buzz reached for the door.

CHAPTER NINETEEN

"Sweet," Doc said, looking around the trailer. "We should get one of these."

"Mom hates camping," Abby said.

"Yeah, but this is way nicer than a tent."

There was a stove and fridge, bunk beds, chairs, and a table bolted to the floor. Three clean blue flight suits lay on the table.

Buzz grabbed one and stepped into the closet-size bathroom.

"As soon as we talk to the president, the doctors will come in," Buzz said as he changed. "You two might want to think about heading home."

"Not until we help fix things," Abby said.

Buzz came out of the bathroom, zipping up his suit.

"Thanks," he said. "You guys have guts."

"Almost time," Doc said, looking out a window in the side of the trailer.

Hundreds of sailors lined up outside the trailer. The seats were full of men in suits. The musicians stood, holding their instruments.

"Hey," Doc said, pointing. "Look who's here!"

Standing with the band—towering above them—was Abraham Lincoln. He was wearing a white navy uniform. The pants didn't reach his shoes. He was holding a tuba. It looked like he might be trying to figure out how it worked.

"*Him* again," Buzz muttered.

"He's just trying to help," Abby said.

"How?" Buzz wanted to know.

"Here they come!" Doc said.

He and Abby ducked under the table—hoping they were out of sight.

The crowd cheered as three figures in bulky gray BIGs marched toward the trailer. The cameras were rolling, and millions were watching live on TV.

Everything looked normal.

A sailor opened the door of the trailer, and Neil Armstrong, Nat Love, and Mike Collins stepped in. The door shut behind them.

Buzz Aldrin said, "Welcome home, cowboys."

"Wish you could have been there," Neil said.

"Me too," said Buzz.

Neil, Mike, and Nat stripped off their gas masks and BIGs. Neil and Mike pulled on their flight suits.

The marching band struck up "Hail to the Chief." President Nixon started toward the trailer.

"Shove over," Nat said, crowding in with Doc and Abby under the table.

Nixon stood in front of the trailer's back window.

Neil Armstrong, Buzz Aldrin, and Michael Collins appeared in the window, smiling and waving.

"Neil, Buzz, and Mike," the president began, "I want you to know that I think I'm the luckiest man in the world. And I say this not only because I have the honor to be president of the United States, but particularly because I have the privilege of speaking for so many in welcoming you back to Earth."

Under the table, Doc and Abby shook hands.

"Our work is done," Doc whispered.

"Time to go," Abby said. "You ready, Nat?"

"Ready for a steak," Nat said. "And a bath. And a week of sleep."

"Okay," Doc said. "Let's sing."

Quietly, they sang:

Nothing happened. They were still under the table.

"A little bit louder?" Abby whispered.

They sang a little louder.

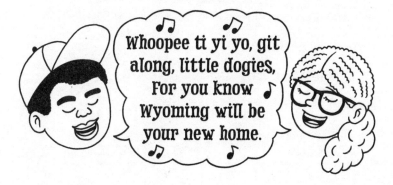

Nothing.

Except that President Nixon leaned closer to the window.

"What's that strange sound?" he asked.

CHAPTER TWENTY

The president got right up to the window, cupping his hands around his eyes to get a better view.

You fellas bring back an alien?

he asked, laughing.

"I don't think so, Mr. President," Neil said.

Buzz turned and motioned for Nat, Doc, and Abby to get lower.

"Something's moving in there!" Nixon

shouted. "I just saw something under the—"

BRRRROOOOOOOOOOPPPP!

A tuba blast cut the president short. Nixon turned toward the awful noise.

"Sorry," Abraham Lincoln said, tapping his tuba.

Nixon looked Lincoln up and down.

"You need a shave, sailor," Nixon said.

"Yes, sir."

"And music lessons."

"Agreed, sir."

Nixon smiled. "Funny, you look a bit like my favorite president."

The bandleader stepped forward. "Excuse me, Mr. President. This man is not in the band."

"Yeah, and he took my tuba," the tuba player said.

"Sorry, son," Lincoln said. He handed back the tuba.

Secret Service agents surrounded Lincoln, blocking Nixon's view of the trailer window.

"I told you Lincoln would help," Abby said.

"He bought us a few seconds," Doc agreed. "But the song's not working."

"Hurry, guys," Buzz whispered.

"We have to try something else," Abby said. "What's worked before?"

Doc snapped his fingers. "Last time, with Abigail Adams, it was her famous line— 'Remember the ladies.'"

"Right!" Abby said. "Maybe something like that would work now."

"They're taking Lincoln away," Buzz whispered. "Hurry!"

"Neil had a great line," Nat said. "When he first stepped on the moon."

"We heard it," Doc said.

"Let's try it!" said Abby.

And they all said together:

THAT'S ONE SMALL STEP FOR MAN, ONE GIANT LEAP FOR MANKIND!

And they were gone.

Doc and Abby tumbled out of the cardboard box in the storage room behind their school library.

They opened the storage room door and walked through the library. Ms. Ventura was at the front desk, checking out books for first graders. She looked up.

"I hope you weren't looking for a book that entire time, Doc."

"Not exactly," Doc said.

"Well, if you want to take something, make sure to check it out," the librarian said. She seemed a tiny bit annoyed.

"Of course," Abby said.

"I'm not saying it was you guys," Ms. Ventura said. "But a lot of books have gone missing lately."

She went back to helping the first graders. Doc and Abby walked back to their classroom.

Doc yawned. "Fixing history is really tiring."

"I know," Abby agreed. "Maybe nothing else will break."

"Let's hope," Doc said. "But somehow I doubt it. Abe Lincoln thinks someone's messing with history."

"Who?"

"He didn't say," Doc said. "He doesn't know. I hope he got home all right."

"He always does," Abby said. "I hope he never plays the tuba again."

"That too," Doc said.

They opened their classroom door.

Everyone gazed up at them—with shock and wonder.

"Nice of you two to join us," Ms. Maybee said. She seemed more amazed than angry. "We've been following your adventures in our books."

All the kids had history textbooks open on their desks.

"We're supposed to be doing math," Ms. Maybee told Abby and Doc. "But they're refusing to put their history books away."

"That's a first," Doc said as he fell into his seat.

"No kidding," said Ms. Maybee.

"Nat Love's back with the cowboys in

Texas!" Carter shouted, reading from his book.

"Oh, good," Abby said. She dropped into her seat and rested her head on her desk.

Kids started asking questions:

WAS THAT REALLY YOU GUYS? IN HISTORY?

HOW'D YOU GET THERE?

CAN WE GO, TOO?

"Abby? Doc?" Ms. Maybee said. "Would you care to explain?"

But they were both asleep.

"All right," Ms. Maybee sighed. "Some other time, then." She checked the clock on the wall. "Let's go to recess."

"No!" the kids shouted.

Ms. Maybee stood with her hands on her hips. "What do you mean, *no*? Every day you whine to me, '*When's recess? We need more recess!*'"

"We don't want recess anymore," Carter said.

All around him, kids were flipping through their history books.

Ms. Maybee could not believe her eyes. "What *do* you want?"

And the class—those that were awake—shouted,

MORE HISTORY!

UN-TWISTING HISTORY

I'm like the kids in Doc and Abby's class—I
was not always a big history fan. But I *was*
always into reading about cowboys and
astronauts. So why not combine them in one
book?

And the two jobs actually have a lot in
common. Both sound fun but were actually
brutally hard and demanding. Both cowboys
and astronauts had to be small or average
size, strong, super fit, and cool under
pressure. Both went on long, dangerous,
lonely journeys with bad food, not enough
sleep, and no one around to help when things
went wrong. It's no coincidence that the first
astronauts were often referred to as "space
cowboys."

In terms of what was real in this story and

what was made up, I'll start with the cowboys.

Nat Love was one of the most famous cowboys in American history. As he describes to Neil Armstrong in chapter 8, he was born into slavery in Tennessee and headed west at fifteen looking for work and adventure. Nat met up with a group of Texas cowboys on the streets of Dodge City, Kansas, and was struck by the fact that a few of the cowboys were African American. He asked to join. The boss said he could—if he could ride a wild horse. The cowboys brought the horse. Nat jumped on. "This proved the worst horse to ride I had ever mounted in my life," Love would later write in his autobiography, *The Life and Adventures of Nat Love*, "but I stayed with him and the cowboys were the most surprised outfit you ever saw, as they had taken me for a tenderfoot, pure and simple."

Nat was hired for thirty dollars a month. He spent the next twenty years riding the trails, winning fame for his roping, marksmanship, and skill with horses. Like all cowboys, Nat preferred not to get off his horse unless he had to. Once, he even rode into a saloon. He ordered two drinks. One for himself and one for the horse.

And he did his share of singing. Cowboys really did sing to their herds at night. In their experience, it was the best way to keep the cattle calm.

Would Nat Love have made a good astronaut?

I definitely think so—with the right training. The first American astronauts were all military jet pilots with at least fifteen hundred hours of flight time, *and* they had advanced science and engineering degrees. So it's fair to say teenage Nat wouldn't have been quite ready.

Nat would have stood out for another reason, too—in 1969, every single American astronaut was white and male. Black men, and women for that matter, simply did not have an equal chance to get the kind of flying experience and elite education needed to qualify for astronaut training.

In the years since the first moon landing, things began to change. Air Force pilot and aerospace engineer Guy Bluford was one of three African American men accepted to NASA's astronaut class of 1978. In 1983, at the controls of Space Shuttle *Challenger*, Bluford made history as the first African American in space. Sally Ride became the first American woman in space that same year.

GUY BLUFORD   **SALLY RIDE**

What about all the space action in this book? How much of that was real?

Well, you probably know that Buzz Aldrin was actually the second man on the moon—not Nat Love. Another totally made-up thing: In this story, the lunar module *Eagle* lands and takes off a couple of times. That could never have happened. The *Eagle* was designed to land just once. And it had enough fuel to blast only the top half of the craft up from the surface of the moon, leaving its long spider legs behind.

Still, a lot of the history and science in this book is pretty realistic.

When it came to exploring space, the United States really was behind Russia. In 1961, President John F. Kennedy boldly challenged Americans to take the lead, saying: "I believe that this nation should commit itself to achieving the goal, before the decade is out, of landing a man on the moon and returning him safely to Earth."

That sparked the race to the moon. NASA gave the name "Apollo" to the series of missions designed to meet Kennedy's goal. On each Apollo mission, NASA engineers and astronauts tested equipment and practiced skills they'd need to make it to the moon and back. In July 1969, with Neil Armstrong in command, *Apollo 11* blasted off and headed for the moon.

Armstrong grew up in Ohio, a nerdy (I mean that as a compliment) kid whose idea of fun was to test model airplanes in the wind tunnel he built in his family's basement. He learned to fly a plane at fifteen, before he could even drive a car. At twenty, he flew fighter jets in the Korean War. Thirty-eight years old at the time of the *Apollo 11* launch, he had the ideal combination of brains, talent, and nerves to lead the mission.

As Edwin "Buzz" Aldrin told Doc and Abby,

he grew up in New Jersey. He got his famous nickname from his younger sister, who, as a toddler, couldn't pronounce his real name. She tried to call him "Brother" instead, but it came out "Buzzer." The family shortened it to Buzz, and the name stuck. A fighter pilot with a PhD in aeronautics from MIT, Buzz had the classic astronaut mix of over-the-top skills and smarts. And, understandably, he really did want to be first on the moon.

He'd probably hate this story, where he doesn't get to go at all. Sorry, Buzz.

The action of the moon landing was so thrilling I didn't need to invent new details. The *Eagle*'s computers really did crash during the descent, and the planned landing site actually was full of craters and boulders. With alarms sounding and only seconds of fuel remaining, Armstrong calmly piloted the craft to a safe spot.

The entire computing power of *Eagle*, by

the way, could easily be replaced by a single smartphone.

I relied heavily on actual transcripts of the conversations between the astronauts and Mission Control in Houston. I even used a lot of the real dialogue. Neil's first words from the moon really were, "Houston, Tranquility Base here. The *Eagle* has landed." CapCom Charles Duke's response was, "Roger, Tranquility. We copy you on the ground. You've got a bunch of guys about to turn blue. We're breathing again. Thanks a lot."

As he climbed down from *Eagle*, Buzz (not Nat, as I have it in this story) really did joke about getting locked out. Buzz Aldrin may not have been first to walk on the moon, but he was first to crack a joke on the moon.

Neil and Buzz collected rock samples, did scientific experiments, set up an American flag, and talked to President Richard Nixon. They took off, docked with Michael Collins on *Columbia*, flew home, splashed down in the Pacific, and were picked up by the aircraft carrier *Hornet*, where they were greeted by the president. Fear of moon germs and the use of Biological Isolation Garments and the isolation trailer were real. Turns out there were no moon germs.

If you must know, a terrible smell really did waft from the *Columbia* capsule when it was first opened. Blame the combination of no showers and a gas-producing diet. As Buzz later said, "We could have shut down our altitude-control thrusters and done the job ourselves."

Finally, about Armstrong's "One small step" line.

It's one of the most famous quotes in human history, and rightfully so. But we still don't know exactly what he said. Armstrong definitely meant to say, "That's one small step for a man, one giant leap for mankind."

"I rehearsed it that way," he later said. "I meant it that way."

But when you listen to the recording, there's no *a*. Maybe, in all the excitement, he forgot the *a*. Or maybe the little word got lost in the 240,000-mile transmission to Earth.

I agree with Doc. Either way, it's a great line.

CREDITS

STEVE SHEINKIN, *Author*

NEIL SWAAB, *Interior Illustrator / Designer*

OLIVIA ASERR, *Cover Illustrator*

MIKE BURROUGHS, *Cover Letterer*

CONNIE HSU, *Executive Editor*

JENNIFER BESSER, *Publisher*

ELIZABETH CLARK, *Creative Director*

TOM NAU, *Director of Production*

JILL FRESHNEY, *Senior Executive Managing Editor*

MEGAN ABBATE, *Assistant Editor*

What did you want to be when you grew up? My younger brother and I spent most of our childhood writing stories and making "shows"—comedy sketches that we'd videotape. I've seen some of the tapes recently. They're not that funny. But we thought they were, and I became convinced I was going to be some kind of writer.

What's your most embarrassing childhood memory? I cried pretty much the entire first day of first grade. It was a new school, and I really didn't want to be there. A lot of kids, even my friends, never let me forget that day . . .

What's your favorite childhood memory? I once got a metal detector as a present, and it was so exciting to use it in my yard. I was absolutely sure I'd find buried treasure! I didn't. But still, to this day I can't resist any story about buried treasure.

What was your favorite thing about school? When a teacher would tell us stories. I didn't care if it was a fictional epic like *The Odyssey*, or something from history, or just a true story from the teacher's own life. Almost any story at all held my attention.

Did you play sports as a kid? I always loved playing sports with friends, but was never super serious about being on teams. In middle school and high school I was on the cross-country team, because that was one sport that welcomed the very skinny.

What was your first job, and what was your "worst" job? I've had so many terrible jobs, far too many to list, and that's one reason I'm so happy now being a writer. I started with the usual lawn mowing. To me, the worst jobs were in restaurants, where you had to act happy in front of the customers. My bosses kept telling me, "You don't smile enough!"

How did you celebrate publishing your first book? The day I found out my first book was going to be published was the *exact* same day I found out my wife and I were going to have a daughter. So the daughter news sort of won out, and rightfully so.

Where do you write your books? I used to go to my public library. I'd sit in the exact same seat and stay there all day. After I had a few books published, I was able to afford to rent a tiny office. I like getting out of the house, because I feel like I'm really going to work.

What sparked your imagination for the Time Twisters series? Well, I don't like to admit it, because I'm afraid kids will get mad, but I used to write history textbooks for a living. I always felt sorry for the historical figures who were stuck in those boring books, doing the same thing over and over. That led to the idea of letting them escape and go on adventures in other times and places.

What challenges do you face in the writing process, and how

do you overcome them? As much as I love my job, I do think the writing process is pretty hard. It takes a lot of discipline to put in the hours needed to write something good.

What's the best advice you have ever received about writing? "Keep going." It sounds so simple, but it's the hardest part. Just keep working, no matter what.

What would you do if you ever stopped writing? At this point, I'm not really qualified to do anything else.

If you could live in any fictional world, what would it be? I'd want to be on a pirate ship of some kind, like in one of my favorite books, *Treasure Island*. I know real-life pirates were cruel and disgusting, but in fictional adventures it seems like a lot of fun.

If you could travel in time, where would you go and what would you do? This fantasy is such a key part of the Time Twisters. I get to send my characters to meet people like Abe Lincoln and Amelia Earhart, to ride with cowboys and see the ancient Olympics. A big part of making up the stories is asking myself, "Where would you like to go next?"

If you were a superhero, what would your superpower be? Funny you should ask, because my daughter and I have been talking about this over breakfast and we came up with a great one. And by "great" I mean hilariously lame. It's Non-Fiction Man! He has the power to convince kids history is exciting! At least, he thinks he does. He and his daughter set out on adventures, and of course things go terribly wrong . . .

STEVE SHEINKIN used to write textbooks, and he's very sorry about that. But now he writes good books, like *Undefeated, Most Dangerous, The Port Chicago 50, Bomb,* and *The Notorious Benedict Arnold.* He's a three-time National Book Award Finalist and has won a Newbery Honor. Steve lives with his family in Saratoga Springs, New York. **stevesheinkin.com**

OH NO! FAMOUS FOLKS FROM HISTORY
KNOW THEY DON'T HAVE TO DO THE SAME
OLD THING ANYMORE—AND EVERYTHING IS
TWISTING OUT OF CONTROL!

FIND OUT WHAT HAPPENS IN THE OTHER
TIME TWISTERS ADVENTURES:

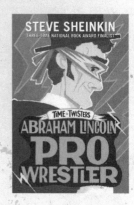  

KEEP READING FOR AN EXCERPT FROM
AMELIA EARHART AND THE FLYING CHARIOT . . .

CHAPTER ONE

The bell rang. The kids cheered.

"Okay, guys," Ms. Maybee told her fourth-grade class, "see you Monday!"

Everyone got up and started shoving stuff into backpacks. Except for Abby and Doc. They stayed slumped in their chairs.

ABBY.
SHE ONCE HELPED NEIL ARMSTRONG LAND ON THE MOON.

DOC.
HE WAS ONCE A LOOKOUT ON A PIRATE SHIP. (HE WASN'T VERY GOOD.)

Between school, soccer, and fixing history, it had been a tiring week.

Ms. Maybee walked up to them. "I know I'm fascinating, but you really do have to leave."

Abby yawned. Doc nodded sleepily.

They stumbled toward the library, eyes half closed. They shuffled past the checkout desk.

"Abby and Doc! The ones who broke history!"

That woke them up a bit. They turned to see who'd spoken.

It was a girl. About nine, their age. She stood in front of the librarian's bulletin board, which was filled with photos of students in their Halloween costumes.

Hi, I'm Sarah, but everyone calls me Sally.

the girl said, speaking in quick bursts.

"I'm homeschooled, but they let me use the library. I've heard about the strange things that have been happening. Abe Lincoln becoming a pro wrestler! Abigail Adams on a pirate ship! It *was* you, right? The ones who broke history?"

"It was really more Lincoln's fault," Doc said.

"That's what I heard," Sally said.

"We've been trying to fix things," Abby said.

"Must be fun!" Sally shouted.

Abby and Doc looked at each other. They weren't sure if they were supposed to talk about this. And anyway, they didn't have the energy to explain.

"Well, it was nice to meet you," Abby said.

"Yeah," Doc said. "See you."

They trudged between tall shelves to the back of the library.

Sally followed. "Where are you going

now? The Wild West? King Arthur's Court?"

"We're going to wait for our mom," Doc said.

"Oh."

They stopped in front of the door to the storage room.

"She's a teacher here," Abby said. "We sit back in this storage room after school, do homework and stuff, till she's ready to leave."

Sally smiled. "Well, guess I'll get back to my reading. See you later?"

"Yeah," Doc said, yawning. "Sure."

Abby and Doc went into the storage room and shut the door. The small space had bookshelves, a table, two chairs, and a tall cardboard box that somehow took Abby and Doc to times and places they read about in history class.

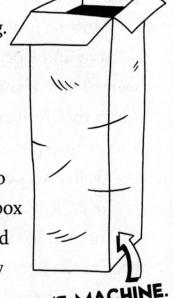

TIME MACHINE.
(SERIOUSLY.)

People from history could use the box, too. That's how all the trouble began. Abraham Lincoln had jumped out of the box and announced he was quitting history—and became a pro wrestler instead. Doc and Abby convinced him to go back to being president of the United States. But other people from history saw what Lincoln had done. If Lincoln could travel through time, so could they. Abigail Adams, the first lady, joined a pirate ship. The cowboy Nat Love flew to the moon.

Getting everyone back where they belonged was exhausting. All Doc and Abby wanted to do now was rest.

They threw down their backpacks and fell into the chairs. Abby took off her glasses, folded her arms on the table, and rested her head in her arms. Doc put his feet up on the table and tilted his head back. His baseball hat dropped to the floor.

They both closed their eyes, hoping for a nice long nap.

Which they would not get.

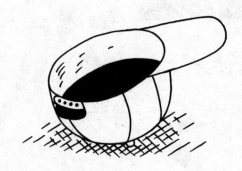

CHAPTER TWO

"**W**ake up, sleepyheads! Time to go home!"
Doc's chair tipped back, and he crashed to the floor.

"Whaaaa?" Abby groaned, wiping drool from her mouth. "Oh, hi, Mom."

Their mom stood in the doorway. She laughed.

> Looks like you two have been hard at work.

"It's Friday," said Doc, lying flat on his back. "No homework."

Abby reached for her glasses.

They weren't there.

Instead, right where she'd left the glasses was a pair of goggles.

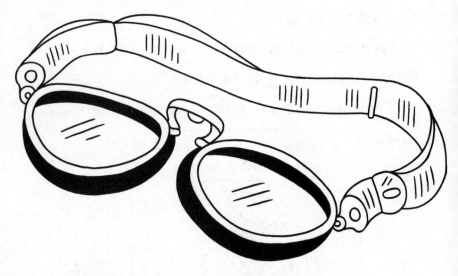

"What?" Abby asked. "Where are my glasses?"

"And my hat," Doc said, looking around. "Where's my hat?"

"Abigail," their mom said, "*please* tell me you did not lose your glasses."

"I didn't!"

"Where are they?"

"I don't know."

"That's the definition of *lost*, last I checked." Their mom sighed. "Do you still have that old pair in your bag?"

"I hate those," Abby moaned.

"Just till you find your good ones. Get your stuff together, both of you, and meet me in my classroom."

Abby reached into a pocket in her backpack and pulled out the glasses she'd gotten in kindergarten. They had goofy tiger-stripe frames. She put them on.

Abby picked up the goggles. They looked like the kind pilots wore in the early days of airplanes. They sort of reminded her of Amelia Earhart's flight goggles.

Abby was a big fan of Amelia Earhart, the famous pilot. She'd been Amelia for Halloween, and her costume had come with goggles just like these. But those were cheap plastic. These were much heavier, with glass lenses and metal frames.

Trick or treat!

She put the goggles on over her glasses. The canvas strap was loose, as if it had been adjusted to fit a bigger head.

"Look at this," Doc said, touching the back of the strap. On the strap, in black ink, were two letters:

"That's how Amelia Earhart signed letters: *AE*," Abby said.

"Could they be real?" Doc wondered. "Really Amelia's?"

"Things *have* been getting mixed up lately," Abby pointed out.

"Yeah, but mostly people from history. Not, you know, eyewear."

They both looked at the tall cardboard box.

Abby walked to the box. She tilted it toward her and looked in.

"No glasses in here," Abby said.

"How about my hat?"

"Just a few history books at the bottom. Same as always."

Abby stepped onto a chair, then up onto the table. From there, she stepped up to the top of a wobbly stack of boxes. She tightened the strap on the pilot goggles.

"Mind if I ask what you're doing?" Doc said.

"I need to give these back," Abby said,

tapping the goggles. "And see if she has my glasses."

"Why would Amelia Earhart have your glasses?" Doc asked.

"I don't know, but Mom's gonna be mad if I can't find them," Abby said. "Plus, I always wanted to meet her."

"I don't think that's what the cardboard box is for."

"Okay, box," Abby said. "I'm not sure exactly where Amelia Earhart is right now, but hopefully you know, so um . . . yeah, thanks."

She bent her knees and jumped toward the tall box. She flew in feet first—and disappeared without a sound.